The Greedy Old Fat Man

an American folk tale
retold and illustrated by

PAUL GALDONE

CLARION BOOKS

Ticknor & Fields: A Houghton Mifflin Company

NEW YORK

For Candi and Sybil

Clarion Books
Ticknor & Fields, a Houghton Mifflin Company

Copyright © 1983 by Paul Galdone

Printed in the U.S.A.
H 10 9 8 7 6 5 4 3 2 1

Library of Congress Cataloging in Publication Data
Galdone, Paul.   The greedy old fat man.
Summary: In this adaptation of an American folktale,
a greedy fat man eats everything in sight, including a
cat, a dog, a rabbit, even a little boy and girl, until
a clever squirrel gets the best of him and frees them.
[1. Folklore—United States]   I. Title.
PZ8.1.G15Gr   1983   3.98.2′1′0973   [E]   83-2057
ISBN 0-89919-188-6

nce there was a greedy old fat man who could never get enough to eat. He got up one morning and ate a hundred biscuits and drank a barrel of milk, and still he was hungry.

He went out of his house and soon he met a little boy and girl.

The little boy said, "Old man, what makes you so fat?"

"I ate a hundred biscuits and I drank a barrel of milk, and I'll eat you, too, if I can catch you!"

So he chased after the little boy and girl, and caught them, and ate them. And then he went on till he met a little dog.

The little dog said, "Old man, what makes you so fat?"
   "I ate a hundred biscuits, I drank a barrel of milk,
I ate a little boy, I ate a little girl, and I'll eat you, too, if
I can catch you."

So he chased after the little dog, and caught him, and ate him. And then he went on till he met a little cat.

The little cat said, "Old man, what makes you so fat?"
"I ate a hundred biscuits, I drank a barrel of milk,
I ate a little boy, I ate a little girl, I ate a little dog, and
I'll eat you, too, if I can catch you."

So he chased after the little cat, and caught him, and ate him. And then he went on till he met a little fox.

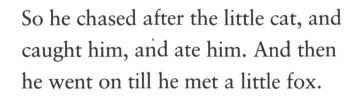

The little fox said, "Old man, what makes you so fat?"

"I ate a hundred biscuits, I drank a barrel of milk, I ate a little boy, I ate a little girl, I ate a little dog, I ate a little cat, and I'll eat you, too, if I can catch you."

So he chased after the little fox, and caught him, and ate him. And then he went on till he met some little rabbits.

One little rabbit said, "Old man, what makes you so fat?"

"I ate a hundred biscuits, I drank a barrel of milk, I ate a little boy, I ate a little girl, I ate a little dog, I ate a little cat, I ate a little fox, and I'll eat you, too, if I can catch you."

So he chased after the little rabbits, and caught them, and ate them. And then he went on till he met a little squirrel.

The little squirrel said, "Old man, what makes you so fat?"

"I ate a hundred biscuits, I drank a barrel of milk, I ate a little boy, I ate a little girl, I ate a little dog, I ate a little cat, I ate a little fox, I ate some little rabbits, and I'll eat you, too, if I can catch you."

The little squirrel said, "You can't catch me, old man," and he ran up a tree. The old man climbed up after him.

The squirrel ran out on a limb, and the old man followed him. The squirrel jumped over to another tree, and the old man tried to jump, too. But he dropped to the ground and broke wide open.

The little boy said, "I'm out!"
The little girl said, "I'm out!"
The little dog said, "I'm out!"

The little cat said, "I'm out!"
The little fox said, "I'm out!"
The little rabbits said, "We're out!"

And the little squirrel said, "I'm out, too, because I wasn't ever in!"